J. F C.

Poems and Essays: Inspirational

J. F C.

Poems and Essays: Inspirational

ISBN/EAN: 9783337246617

Printed in Europe, USA, Canada, Australia, Japan

Cover: Foto ©Andreas Hilbeck / pixelio.de

More available books at **www.hansebooks.com**

Poems and Essays:

INSPIRATIONAL.

BY J. F. C.

———∞———

SYRACUSE, N. Y.:

MASTERS & LEE, STEAM BOOK AND JOB PRINTERS.

1867.

TO THE READER.

THIS work is respectfully dedicated to those, who appreciating the Natural Laws of God, like to study manifestations of Love and Wisdom, as they are exhibited through Matter and Spirit.

As these Inspirations have instructed and cheered the writer, so may they comfort the reader, until divested of the Material Casket, we become better prepared to test their truthfulness.

CONTENTS.

PART FIRST.

PART SECOND.

PART THIRD.

SPIRIT VOICES FROM THE BELOVED DEPARTED TO SURVIVING FRIENDS.

THE BIRTH-DAY GIFT.

Years pass ! and friends to thee would give
  Some token of their love :
And those, who from the mortal sight,
  Have passed to courts above,

Around thee linger as of old,
  Some gift they would impart :
They cannot bring an outward gift,
  As token of the heart.

But light immortal they would shed,
  And truth to guide thy feet,
Until in brighter realms above,
  The friends long parted meet.

Then press thy way through birth-days here,
  To brighter birth above :
Where heaven's richer gifts shall shower
  On thee in light and love.

———+ +———

A SONG OF THE BEREAVED.

Where are the friends whom oft I greeted,
  And who on me such love bestowed ?
Whose well known footsteps, ever welcome,
  Increased my joy, and quelled my woes ?

Where is the brother, whom in childhood,
  I loved with heart so kind and true?
Who proudly spoke the name of sister,
  More proudly, as we older grew?

Alas! They're gone! Sometimes in sadness
  I think upon the days, passed by;
And dwell on those sweet hours of gladness,
  Until I breathe the rising sigh:

And feel almost alone, deserted,
  By the dear loved ones of the past;
O! were it not for truth immortal,
  Cheering my soul by clouds o'ercast,

And opening to my spirit yearnings,
  A world all radiant with delight,
Those sad, dark hours would linger longer,
  And overwhelm me with their blight.

But ah, the morning dawns upon me!
  Friends of my childhood, linger near;
Though they long, long ago departed,
  They still return my soul to cheer.

And messages of peace they bring me
  From the bright land beyond the sea,
Of discord, passion, darkness, sorrow;
  They come to make my spirit free.

And the dear brother is not absent,
  Though still unseen, he lingers near,
He fain would see his sister happy:
  He fain would quell each rising fear,

And see her soul all full of music,
  Harmonious with the spheres above ;
Where discord from *his* soul is banished,
  By the bright reign of peace and love.

——‡‡——

CONSOLATION.

Know you not that all is passing,
  Changing, fleeting, like a dream ;
That beyond this world of sorrow,
  Ever changing is the scene ?

Yet true friendship is not fickle ;
  True love cannot pass away.
Chastened heart, ever remember,
  Change gives place to brighter day.

Though some loved ones have departed,
  They are dwelling in the light ;
Ever changing in condition,
  Makes them beautiful and bright.

Upward rising, onward fleeing,
  From the weight their souls did bear ;
Know you not that sweet communion
  Can be had with them by prayer ?

Prayer shall dissipate the distance,
  Trust and love will bring them near ;
Let not anguish rend your spirit,
  Upward press without a fear.

Soon the pearly gates will open,
  Then true souls will fully blend.
Cheerfully and lovingly,
  Pass along.   Your angel friends.

Of your sorrows not unmindful,
  Wait to help you on your way.
O ! believe that truly, surely,
  They approach to those who pray.

———‡‡———

FRIENDSHIP IMMORTAL.

Do not withdraw the Friendship
  Which you to me have given ;
It is a chain to bind us,
  More firmly to that heaven
From which pure souls descended,
  To dwell in forms of clay.
O ! then in sweet communion,
  We'll work on day by day.

Though absent oft in body,
  We're one in spirit still ;
The same pure inspiration
  Our waiting souls does fill.
While Christ and holy angels,
  Do beckon us to rise
To those divine conditions,
  Where friendship never dies.

PROGRESS.

This life, so brief and fleeting ;
  By our spirits active made ;
Is ever onward tending
  To that life beyond the shade.
Death does not change the spirit :
  But its surroundings change ;
And in its new condition,
  It has a wider range.

Departed ones are with us ;
  Only, with deeper love,
And wiser, holier impulse,
  They on our souls do move.
They fain would lead our spirits,
  To the loves which angels bless :
They're with us now as ever,
  Only with holier caress.

And drear, dark spirits linger,
  Around this world of ours ;
We should not let them lead us,
  To passion's withered bowers ;
But we with strength of spirit,
  Should labor to impress,
The weary ones, corrupted,
  And lead them unto rest,

The rest which none but loving,
  Obedient souls do know ;
The rest, which in well doing,
  Great joy on us bestows.

The rest, which here does give us,
 A foretaste of that joy,
Prepared for the obedient,
 In spheres without alloy.

———✦✦———

REMINISCENCE.

I've been dreaming, wildly dreaming
 Of the bright days, past and gone ;
When so much of life that's real,
 Only bore for me the thorn.

What is life when spent in sadness,
 When no joy the heart can cheer ?
When our cherished loved ones,
 Cannot dry our bitter tears ?

I will weep no more, nor murmur ;
 Time once spent who would recall ?
But the present, the true present,
 Is within the reach of all.

Gratefully I'll grasp its fullness,
 I am stronger in this hour—
Angel visitants attend me,
 And my soul with hope empower.

In the present, the true present,
 I will live, and act, and love ;
Not alone in purpose striving,
 Ever aided from above,

I will wend my way in gladness,
　　Strewing flowers where were thorns,
Helping disappointed mortals,
　　To outride Earth's darkest storms.

———✦✦———

LIFE HAS JOYS YOU HAVE NOT TASTED

Life has joys you have not tasted :
　　Life has sweets you have not known :
Yet the buds of love and wisdom,
　　On strange winds to you have flown.

Cherish them, for they are sacred,
　　They will open into flowers :
Flowers of precious, holy fragrance,
　　Cheering all your fleeting hours.

Had life been a scene of pleasure,
　　Spent in friendship's sacred bowers,
Where a just appreciation
　　Hallowed every passing hour.

The dear friend whom you've attracted
　　To your home, for thought and rest,
Could not left her bower of pleasure,
　　To become your grateful guest.

And the buds which she has brought you,
　　Have been borne on sorrow's tide,
By strange winds, till they have clustered
　　Closely, closely by your side.

Thus God's agents of progression,
    Are of earthly goods deprived,
That condition may attract them,
    To become the faithful guides,

Of the suffering, human beings,
    Who have strayed from paths of joy ;
For the buds of love and wisdom,
    Blessing give without alloy.

O ! be bright with hope o'erflowing,
    Life has yet a zest for you ;
Precious joys which never weary,
    Gems of truth forever new.

ROB NOT THAT HEART.

Rob not that heart by care oppressed,   .
    To you its fondest throbs were given,
Ere time's rough storms had bowed the head,
    By breaking the bright dream of heaven.

It may not be ! The love she bore
    For you, when in your youthful prime,
Has shone with clear, unceasing ray,
    Up to this day, of life's decline.

O ! twine for her the halcyon wreath,
    Of true devotion ; brighter far
To woman's heart of tenderness,
    Than moon, or sun, or glittering star.

Onward and upward press your way,
    To where frail passions cease control ;
Where love, renewed in innocence,
    Confirms the ties of youthful souls.

———+·+———

SWEET MEMORIES.

It seems but a few days since I was a child,
And gathered with sister, flowers growing wild
By the banks of the stream, which flowed so free :
Then care was a stranger to her and to me.

Our dog and pussy seemed to take delight
In joining our slow walk, or quite rapid flight ;
And when the hills echoed with our merry shout,
They looked, as if asking, What laughing about ?

We picked boquets by the banks of the stream,
And bore them to mother, who with air serene,
Saluted her children's return with a smile,
Saying you are tired, come rest you awhile,

And then with fresh diligence go to your work,
Finish father's garter, or help make his shirt.
Then kind dog and pussy would watch by our side,
As if they feared evil us might betide.

Or, rather they chose to be by us in work,
When knitting a garter, or making a shirt.
They fancied they formed an important part
In the circle of duties around our hearts.

And when we had finished our stent or more,
We would lay by our work, and roam as before ;
Not as in the morning, over hill and glade,
But in the orchard, by the apple-tree's shade.

Then in the garden we would gather flowers,
Which opened so brightly after showers;
And look at the birds' nest on the big tree;
To see that it still from all evil was free.

These hours so propitious, long since passed away;
Early my sister abandoned the clay,
For a home with bright spirit's of happier clime;
Yet she's my sister and will ever be mine.

I shall join her rambles, where death is not known,
And share in the glories of her brighter home.
May patience and fortitude ever control,
Till I meet sister in the home of my soul.

PART SECOND.

———✳———

Thoughts on

Health, Beauty and Immortality.

THOUGHTS ON HEALTH.

The most desirable thing in this wide world, is a sound mind in a sound body. Of all studies which should engage our attention, the most important is that of human philosophy, or an investigation of those established laws, which operate in each human being, and in his associations with all other human beings.

To fully understand that course of action, which will insure the greatest amount of true happiness, physical, intellectual, moral and spiritual, is to have reached the summit of human knowledge. Who, among the vast multitudes of human teachers, have reached that position?

Among those who claim to be teachers of health and practitioners in medicine, do not the advocates of each system, claim for themselves a degree of skill, which *they* do not fully possess, and for their system a power of preserving or of renewing health, which *it* does not fully possess! However, almost if not every system of practice which gains largely and permanently the sympathies of the people is an improvement on past theories. Hence, may we not hope that health, is by and by to be the established condition of human beings? Any mode of treatment, which can drive corrupt elements from the system, and induce therein a condition favorable to the reception and assimilation of healthful elements, will prove beneficial. Vitality, or the life element, ever seeks to renew itself. But place an individual out of the reach of that which creates vitality, and he cannot be expected to gain it. We derive it from food, air, exercise, rest, sleep, bathing, and association. That system of practice which will regulate all these, will surely promote health.

Health is a term equally applicable to body and mind. Lose in either the balance of action, and you lose health in proportion. Health is the result of equilibrium. Equilibrium is productive of power. It is necessary that power be in proportion to the requisite conditions of the being possessing the power. The healthy babe posseses the requisite power of the babe. It breathes, sleeps, takes nourishment, digests, moves the tiny members of its darling, little frame with perfect facility. The dear little thing does not dream of trouble ; but lives in the enjoyment of the healthful action of its being, until it is mismanaged by unskillful nurses. Prick the body, and you interrupt, in a degree, the natural circulation through the affected part. Jolt it too much and you interrupt the circulation still more; let it get cold, and you occasion a still greater inharmony in the action of some of the delicate organs of life. Treat the baby in this way until you make it quite sick, and the balance of action being destroyed, the healthful baby power will be wanting. It does'nt eat, sleep, laugh, or move as usual, because harmonious action is wanting; some organs being overcharged, and others impoverished by this lack of equilibrium. The baby's face loses its bright tint, its love lit eyes grow dim, its tiny hands, which recently grasped with so much avidity every toy within its reach, fall powerless by its side. Darling child! tears must soon bedew the lifeless casket of your unoffending spirit, unless harmony can be restored throughout the wonderful mechanism of your little frame. How nescessary that all learn of the laws of health. Writers are somewhat inclined to put this responsibility entirely upon the mother; but who knows where in this life of change it may appear. The mother may pass from earth, ere she *could care* for her babe. All should study the laws of health that they may care for themselves, if not required to take especial care of others. Who does not require mending? Who enjoys perfect health? Who does not have to take care to keep the balance? The student exclaims, Oh! how my head aches! I study, and study, but cannot master this and that difficulty. Poor fellow! you are like a man tugging a load which he has not muscular strength to move without overdoing, you are trying to accomplish as much as some of your class-mates who possess twice your capacity of endurance. Rest your brain, if you would increase its power. O! I cannot bear to do that replies the student, I will not be out done. Well then, work away until you loose all power of working and learn wisdom by sad experience. We like to be able to pursue with unremitting diligence the favorite schemes of life; but we must remember that patience is a most essential ingredient in human happiness. We cannot always control the varied circumstances attending us; but we can make the best of them. Do the best we can under existing conditions, and if we cannot do much, we certainly cannot fail of doing well, and of reaping our reward in the possession of a clear conscience and of a mind still more unfolded in wisdom. Some people have a great dread of difficulties: when they find themselves assailed by them, they spend their energies in sorrow, instead of looking for the best course to take. We may avoid unpleasant surroundings when we can; but finding ourselves in them, the grand watchword is not grief but action.

Difficulties prevent our capabilities from stagnating :

they call out our strength and thereby increase it. The greater they become, the more deeply do they make us feel our need of powers above ourselves to inspire us for the conflict; thus fulfilling the glorious purpose of leading us into nearer communion with the spiritual and Omnipotent. If we claim divine assistance under difficulties, we must not act unreasonably, and overtax our natural powers. When by the force of circumstances, over which we have no control, difficulties arise, then may we pray, Father help us! But when with our eyes open, we have run into trouble, we can only regret our error, and pray for strength to refrain in future from the abuse of the natural laws. Man's passional nature has everything to do with his health and happiness ; for when viewed in its broadest sense, it is co-extensive with his being. Thus we hear of a man's possessing a passion for such and such sciences ; for the poetic ; for beauty, wealth, fame. But when the term passional nature, is narrowed to its smallest limits, phrenologically speaking, we confine it to combativeness, destructiveness, alimentiveness, and amitiveness. These elements, in their individual action, seem especially essential to the fulfilling of a part of our earth mission. Yet they are not to act independently of the higher faculties. They cannot without serious detriment to their possessor. The moment that destructiveness gets the start of benevolence, conscience, reason, that moment the individual is out of balance, and reckless of consequences. The moving spring of action being destructiveness, he is impelled to its gratification. Come what may, he is resolved to destroy the object of his resentment. This state of affairs precedes passional murder. In deliberate murder, the *will* acts powerfully with desrtuctiveness. Murderers usually possess large destructiveness with a deficiency of moral development. Who will say that such organizations would not have been improved by proper training? and who will say that the child of such organization, growing in the midst of injurious influences, could really be expected to become a good man or woman? By the strength of every virtue within us, we should seek to benefit such persons, gaining access if possible to the germ of love within, covered as it may be by the rubbish of depravity. Alimentiveness, when not controlled by reason, is destructive of human health. He who eats and drinks immoderately because he likes to, eats and drinks destruction. The food taking faculty being essential to one's existence, growth, and continuance in health, all must exercise that faculty, and should do so with due moderation. In the same manner should we exercise every faculty, if we would not suffer the loss of mental and physical health. Who would be willing to make himself stupid by taking too much or improper food, or who would suffer the abnormal condition occasioned by taking to excess of intoxicating drinks? What reasonable being would be willing thus to pervert his faculties for momentary gratification; and that of a much lower order than the exercise of the higher faculties is capable of yielding? The pleasure of eating moderately is all right, but the enjoyment of excess is a thousand fold overbalanced by the physical and mental suffering occasioned by such excess. How many have been ruined by intemperance? Yet others follow the same dark pathway.

Reason! Reason! Take thy throne and lead men to virtue and to God. Reason beautifully corresponds with the teachings of christianity. Said Jesus "It is written, man shall not live by bread alone; but by every word that proceedeth out of the mouth of God." True! the higher faculties must be fed by the higher food. Eat to nourish the physical, that it may be sustained for the action of the unfolding, ever progressing spirit. The sciences and arts, the divine laws and divine loves, shall feed these higher powers, until it shall be said to the ripened soul " well done thou good and faithful servant, enter into higher joys." The great conditions of health are equilibrium and change. These conditions apply equally to physical and mental organizations. When the receptive or casting off physical powers are weak or diseased, this law of change is violated and equilibrium is lost. So with the mental powers — They, like the physical, require food and exercise. How absurd to think of narrowing the mentality of an individual by keeping him ever in a routine of business, which furnishes perpetual drudgery to his faculties: a routine to which he is not adapted, and for which he has no taste. Such a course is destructive to physical and mental health. The law of change is violated, for the best energies being spent in an uncongenial employment, there is little strength or room for the reception of new and grand ideas on congenial themes. Woman suffers much, very much, by the violation of this law. In the present arrangements of social life, the domestic and fashionable arena do not furnish work enough of the right kind to keep the minds of all women in health. Many are left with only a part of their mentality called into active service. No wonder that listlessness so early writes its impression on them. Dormant faculties except for purposes of rest, never grow vigorous.

Variety is essential to health. This is evident from the fact that we are constituted with varied capacities, not one of which was designed to lie dormant. All should be brought out by the appropriate stimulus. Unmixed literature will not do. Affection, taste, playfulness, should be fully brought out in every character and perfectly tempered by reason. We do not like to hear people talk of *woman* as if it was a necessity of her nature to be all heart or impulse with little reason. If reason is necessary to guard the heart in man, is it less so in woman? Some people seem to contemplate woman as a being of unmixed impulse; full of feeling and sympathy in whatever direction their superior power may choose to call it out,—capable of loving, and doing, and being, what, and only what, men fancy their necessities require. We believe it in every sense true that woman was created for man. It is no less true that she was created by a power that understands man better than he understands himself. Man needs a companion, a help meet, a better half if you choose so to term it, not only in one, two, or three but in all the departments of life. You can no more consistently narrow the sphere of one sex than of the other. Taste and capacity, restrained by moral rectitude are the true guides in the choice of pursuits.

We do not like to hear the phrenologist say to a woman " *you* have a *man's* head," for if we ask him to explain, he replies, "she has large intellectual powers: is capable of planning well, would with her active mind, tire of the monotony of domestic life." Does it follow that large intellectual powers unfit her for the appropriate duties of her sex? We think large intellectual powers in her favor. The more reason the better, when it is balanced by the universal faculties. An unbalanced head is no better in one sex than in the other; a lack of reason in either is equally unfortunate. Woman was created for man; but not merely to administer to his sensuous nature, to cook his food, wash his clothes, and listen to his oracles, until she loses

the little individuality he deigned to award her. Woman
is an individuality, possessing within herself, not only affection, but a world of faculties to be unfolded. She may,
and must, for this is her destiny, walk with man in the arts
and sciences, and governmental, as well as in the affection-
al department. This idea of woman is not the result of
vain ambition; not the misguided opinion of a few of her
sex; but founded in the stern necessities of human nature,
and hence the all wise Father's will concerning her.

We do not like to see people void of the love of adaptation
or suitableness, or in other words, of reason balanced by
conscience and the universal faculties. An individual in
possession of sufficient reason and conscience loves to do
right. No amount of intellectual power, or love of litera-
ry research, can make such a woman neglect her duties.
She will say "it is unreasonable for me to go there, or to
do that, I have imperative duties at home." The law of love
is paramount, and must be fulfilled at all events. If for a
moment she should seek to gratify herself by the neglect
of actual responsibilities, who would not perceive that her
mind was unbalanced? We should say that too little, rather
than too much reason, had unfitted her for the sacred duties
of domestic life. Said a consistent young man, "It would
be my highest pleasure to travel, but it is unreasonable for
me to think of it. I have my way to make unassisted by
father or friends. I am in a business which affords a living, and promises to patient industry, wealth. I have no
prospect of doing so sure a work by traveling. Hence, as
a matter of prudence and right, I shall at present banish
the idea. Some women seem to imagine that they only are
circumscribed in choice of pursuits. It is not so. Many
men continue in employments not agreeable, because it is
a necessity, or under existing circumstances for the best.

Yet *men* are circumscribed more from other conditions, than from the prejudices of society. Women have been hindered in employments suited to their natural character, because popular opinion cried out "It is no place for woman." So it has been said of her as a lecturer. We ask by what good reason she should be excluded from speaking, either public or private? If ever a being loved to talk, and could talk incessantly without tiring, it is woman. I never supposed conversational proclivities were sins. The immorality or the virtue of talking, consists in the spirit of the words spoken. Consistency is properly styled a jewel. Whatever is best for us to do, we should like to do, though under different circumstances we might choose quite another course. It has been said that whatever is worth doing, is worth doing well. When called to the responsibilities of house-keeping, we should attend to its minutest details: but when out of the employment, the minutia may for a time pass from our minds. If some housekeeper eager to test our knowledge of "woman's sphere," should ask us how to make a good pudding, we need not loose our self-possession, if it takes us longer to remember, than to rehearse the process, after calling it to memory. It simply shows that we have not been idly poring over previous knowledge; but have been feeding the mind in new, and perhaps quite as important fields of thought.

It is not only essential to perfect health, that the body and mind be in themselves harmonious, but also that they be adapted to each other. A strong, capacious mind in a weak body, and a strong body in connection with a weak, inactive mind, seems not the most happy arrangement, and yet such a condition is frequently observable. When the mind is too vigorous for the body, it rapidly exhausts the vital energies. Such a mind should train itself to rest and recreation, until the body has renewed its energies. Are we to suppose the mind ever inactive, or actually asleep? It is frequently unconscious, as it regards the external world. It is so in sleep. Sleep rests the body because the mind ceases to act through the material organization. When we say the mind is tired, do we speak correctly? Should we not say that the organs through which the mind operates are tired? Sleep rests those organs, and the mind acts through them with new vigor. There are instances when mentality seems insufficient for bodily power; such persons should discipline their minds to activity: thus inducing a balance of mental and physical energy. The last named class are liable to suffer physically from a want of action, rather than from too rapid expenditure of vitality. Such should eat moderately, and exercise abundantly. Different constitutions find it necessary to adopt somewhat different habits. When health, mental or physical, is wanting, ascertain where is the lack of equilibrium; restore that, and you restore health. Religionists have sometimes suffered from extreme activity in the organs of conscientiousness and veneration. In this direction, the mind has become so unbalanced as to produce insanity. Hope and imagination are beautiful powers ; but even these may be too large and active to harmonize with other portions of the brain. These, when the basilar brain is deficient, leave people to dwell too much in the aerial regions, for inhabitants of the mundane sphere. However, the *base* of the brain is more liable to be immoderately active. When such is the case, the effect is most unfavorable to the purity, happiness and growth of the individual. The mind should be kept unmarred by the perversions of animality. Then, though from physical weakness, intellect may not manifest its full powers, it will grow vigorous, unfolding more and more until it plumes its bright wings for free skies. Health! Blissful angel! Child of beauty and of love; Sensitive you are; Shrinking from the least rude touch. You dwell with harmony, purity, truth. Whatever disturbs those elements, disturbs you also. Prosperous being; Teach us your laws. Impress us with your matchless worth; Raise us with you to the peerless heavens, where uninterrupted in your ministry, you lead us to the elysian fields of immortality. People sometimes talk of health as if it was a condition distinct from mentality. It cannot be so. The mental and physical existing as they do in intimate relation, act and react on each other. Therefore mental and bodily conditions become doubly important. The physical should be cared for that it may favor mental health. Both important in themselves and doubly so in each other. Inseperable to the gates of death, we should strive to make their companionship mutually profitable.

Says one, "My mind is active, but my poor body keeps me back." Mind, we are sorry for you and for your companion. Try to sustain her until her natural existence shall expire. It is not meet that you despise her. Make her happy if you can. She cannot suffer and leave you exempt therefrom. Cherish her as your best earthly friend. Says another, " My body is pretty well; but my mind is so anxious, I'm sure that my physical being cannot long bear this terrible conflict of mind." You are right. And what a miserable individual is he whose mind and body are both disorderd. For a diseased mind, travel and new and pleasant scenes are a gracious restorative. Do not wait until the body is so affected by mental conditions, that you cannot make her your servant. When you find the mind unsatisfied, gloomy, bitter, seek as the first object to restore her to peace. Minds should not remain uncomfort-

able for lack of employment of the right kind to call out
all their capacities. God made us for progression.

Intellectual gifts are divine, being bounties from the eternal source of intelligence. Dont hide your gifts, they grow
only in feeding and using them. Exercise them, and the
one talent shall become two, and the five talents ten. The
body and mind love to work together. They canot bear to
act in opposition. They love each other and yet by a kind
of mutual misunderstanding, they sometimes disagree.
The body enters into engagements which cramp the mind,
and not having room sufficient to grow as fast as nature in-
tended, she is uneasy and gets the name of being a diffi-
cult, disagreeable personage. Give her room and air, and
all her nature requires, and she'll be well enough. Do not
pamper her with *unsubtsantial* food. Do not oppress her
vitals by *impure* air. Give her just as much proper exercise as her companion, the body, will agree to. Let her
also have society in other minds congenial to her own.
One powerful source of mental growth and discipline, is
proper intercourse with other minds. Self control is a
beautiful result of suitable mental discipline. In a well dis-
ciplined mind, every power acting in its proper place, and
in due degree, greatly promotes physical health. The passions belong in the basement of the soul. It is quite as
much out of place to put them as leading powers, as it is
to build a house with the kitchen, pantry, and wood-shed
in front; such an arrangement would be considered sadly
out of taste and convenience. A man or woman *led* by the
passions is a reproach.

Health has three rules which should be religiously ob-
served. First, Enter into pursuits to which you are or can
become adapted; Second, Cultivate symmetry of develop-

ment, by resting those powers already too active, and bringing out the more dormant. Third, Work and grow bright.

I would not work an atom,
  Said sloth to me one day.
You'll surely loose your courage,
  And faint upon the way.

And there is opposition
  With stern and bitter words.
There's scoffing and derision,
  And many more, In herds.

They follow earnest workers:
  And strew with thorns their paths.
And there is no computing,
  The fierceness of their wrath.

Ah! Sloth you are mistaken,
  If you think them bold and strong.
Before the power of Truth they fall,
  Singing a different song.

Behold *they've* lost their *courage.*
  Truth's weapons bright and fair,
Have torn their ranks asunder,
  And scattered them in air.

INVOCATION.

Jesus, the way, the truth, and the life. Our pattern of
obedience. Like thee may we do the work our Father has
given us to do.

Like thee may we be obedient to every mandate of duty
though it lead us to prison or to death.

Like thee, while we work in the outer world, may we
commune with the spiritual and immortal, that growing in
love and wisdom, we may be prepared for the pursuits and
enjoyments of a higher life.

THOUGHTS ON BEAUTY.

Beauty is an important constituent in orderly creations. We can conceive of it in undying glory and perfection. It is in regions where our Father's laws are perfectly obeyed, that beauty exists unblemished. Yet even here, where man is ever corrupting himself, all the elements or first principles of that beauty exist, which constitutes the attraction of of the celestial and immortal spheres. This has been styled the age of beauty! or rather the commencement of the reign of the love of the beautiful to the exclusion of the supreme reign of the love of mammon. These two ruling powers cannot, in a high degree of development, exist in harmony. The love of riches in gold, except for purposes of beneficence is a dark, withering affection. The love of beauty for its own sake, is elevating to the human soul. The controling influence of the love of wealth may be considered synonomous with the controling influence of selfishness unenlightened. There is an enlightened selfishness, which while it seeks to cultivate, improve and perfect self, fully appreciates the fact that it can do so most effectually by studying and obeying the laws of equality, sympathy, and charity, toward every member of the human race. This course, involving what we from a lack of understanding fully the beautiful arrangements of our heavenly Father, have been wont to consider self-denial, cannot fail of reward ; extending through all future time, crowning the conquering soul with laurels of everlasting beauty. Jesus taught people to take up their cross and follow him as a condition of discipleship. Many, were led to do this in view of the exceeding great reward attending the following of

Jesus. Could this be considered self-denial, or enlightened selfishness ? Is it not the latter ? What are a few short lived pleasures, when weighed in the scale of everlasting joys ? The martyrs of history understood this.

They knew that the wrath of man worketh the righteousness of God. The wrath, putting them to death could be allayed only by the sacrifice of their material existence ! The Father saw that through scenes like these, man would some day emerge into the peaceful arbors of obedience and beauty. Hence for the good of men corrupted, he permitted the temporary sufferings of the righteous. Our Father never designed that we should be willing to suffer, except for the purpose of a higher good to ourselves or to our race.

Good is so diffusive, that it cannot be confined to an individual. I cannot benefit another without benefitting myself. When I give of temporal goods to the needy, I exercise a spirit of good will which enlarges with that exercise, bringing me nearer to him who owns all the treasures of wisdom and knowledge ; and on whom I depend for all that makes me joyous. Martyrs for truth, conferring a great, perpetual benefit on humanity, receive in the unfolding and growth of their spirits, benefit, before which the treasures and joys of this rudimental sphere are as nothing. Yet the enjoyments of our present existence are not to be lightly esteemed : and never sacrificed, except to fulfill the mandates of universal love. Not forgetting the assertion, " Love is the fulfilling of the law. "

Beauty has a close relation to health ; for as perfect health cannot exist without equilibrium, neither can perfect beauty. An insect may feed on the leaves of a healthy rose, interrupting the circulating fluids which naturlly flow so as to create the requisite equilibrium, even of the minutest parts of the plant. The result is not only a loss of the parts eaten, but a withering of the edges of the leaves, and a final destruction of the health and beauty of the flower. So in the human organization : as health declines, beauty, one of the pleasing results of healthful action, gradually fails. " Says one, some very healthy persons are also very homely. " True! It is also true that organizations unbalanced to a great degree, cannot be fully handsome. They often are, from the fine quality of temperament which may characterize them, handsome with exceptions. In criticisms of such, you say, " the head is too large for the body, or the body for the head. The countenance is too restless, or there is a lack of expression. "

Something is ever at fault in really unbalanced temperaments. That well balanced healthful people are sometimes homely, may be attributed to the quality of organization. Such are frequently characterized by dark complexion, coarse skin and hair, and firm muscles. I do not call them homely ; because I see within them admirable elements of power and endurance. I care not how handsome the soul casket may be :

If unaccompanied by an orderly mind, it cannot continue in beauty. If the soul is not kept vigorous and pure, physical beauty loses its charm, even its claim to the title, and becomes like the letter which without the spirit killeth.

Beauty is twofold ; Spiritual and Physical. The casket of the soul in every human being, is originally moulded by the quality and proportions of the soul which it contains ; If the soul is beautiful, and physical balance is perfect, the body will also be beautiful.

Beauty is not only absolute, but relative. An object may be perfect and beautiful in kind, while a higher object is perfect and beautiful in a degree proportionate. The former possessing beauty ; the latter a larger beauty. The violet is beautiful. The rose possesses more wealth of beauty. Though you cannot make the violet more beautiful as a violet, the rose delights you by its more bounteous beauty.

That vicious people sometimes possess a good share of beauty, only proves the elasticity of beauty and that it takes time to destroy it. In fact in its principles and manifestations it is immortal and consequently cannot be destroyed. In its relations and combinations in this material world it may be driven about and almost banished from objects by nature peculiarly its own. Beautiful souls sometimes dwell in bodies, which have not much claim to physical beauty. This is usually attributable to the ravages of disease, and the various causes of inharmony, which afflict us in this rudimental state.

In regions where inharmonies are unknown, are manifestations of ever increasing beauty. We can conceive of every thought there as beautiful in truth : of every sound harmonious in its spirit of beauty ; of every form but the expression of the spiritual idea of beauty. Endless in duration, and infinite in manifestation, it is one of the constituents of the all in all.

We may personify and call it one of the guardian angels of our dark planet earth. Thanking our father for her soothing, refreshing, purifying ministry, we will worship her as an emanation from the eternal.

Those manifestations in the natural world, which especially gratify the organ of sublimity, express more immediately divine power and grandeur, while those which especially gratify ideality, express divine gentleness and love. As power and gentleness ever blend in the divine Father, so grandeur and beauty in the outer world, are

but expressions of the same spiritual elements. Poetry
owes its charm to these elements and may be personified
as a daughter of imagination.

When she assumes a position of power, she is more grand
than gentle. When she robes herself in love she soothes
and sways by gentleness. As an angel of love we address
her as follows :

> Sweet spirit of celestial birth !
> Who has commissioned you to earth ?
> Who bade you wing your radiant way,
> To cheer inhabitants of clay ?
> We know you come from climes above ;
> And that your messages are love,
> Yet you are still a magic spell ;
> Even to hearts that love you well.
> How do you act upon the mind ?
> How yield pleasure so refined ?
> Leading us from earth's toilsome way,
> To sweet, elysian fields of day ?
> Tell us dear spirit ! Then we'll find
> In closer union with your mind,
> Free access to your streams of joy ;
> And drink fresh draughts, without alloy.
> What means that smile upon your face ?
> What means those airs so full of grace ?
> One would suppose you free to tell,
> That we would like to know so well.
> Yet you are silent, radiant one.
> Our questions do not loose your tongue :
> Until you strike a cheerful lay,
> And on your bright wings soar away.
> Henceforth, content then we must be,

To guess fair things concerning you.
To love and cherish you the more,
As seas grow rough and tempest roar.
Thanks to our Father that you come,
To lead us to a brighter home.
We'll not forget your gentle sway,
When on us dawns a clearer day.

We are astonished at the grand, while we love the simply beautiful. The former strikes us with awe, while the latter woos us to her bowers. Persons who possess the element of sublimity larger than ideality, if benevolence and reason do not exert full power, are inclined, in divine worship, to dwell more upon the majesty than the goodness of God.

We should know that we may not judge of the Eternal by the inharmony of our development. We are to view him as a being not unbalanced like ourselves. In aspiring to be like him, we should labor for harmonious, spiritual development. We can feast our imaginations somewhat on the beauty of the unseen sphere. We may also be inspired with infusions of truth therefrom. These inspirations are not to be concealed, or to float in an atmosphere away from human society. They are to be brought home to human understanding, and made to serve man.

Order divine, assert your claim ;
And usher in the glorious day,
Of Beauty's reign.
Truth, Wisdom, Beauty, all agree,
To swell the song of Liberty,
And Peace, Love's daughter
Smiles again in bloom :—

While war expires and sinks into the tomb.
Love's brow grows radiant with delight ;
She joys to see the world all right.

Beauty may not only be abstractly considered, but viewed as a quality entering into relations, and hence dependent upon conditions for self preservation.

In other words, we would say that what is beautifully adapted to one condition, may be quite unsuitable for another, and hence in the relation not beautiful.

Beauty personified is ever the same ; but becomes when viewed as a principle, the counterpart of propriety. Therefore, that which is not suitable under the circumstances, is not beautiful, though under different conditions and entering into different relations, it might be altogether beautiful. To illustrate. An elegant wardrobe appears beautiful on a person in the parlor, but out of taste when on an individual who is scrubbing a kitchen. The dress remains beautiful ; but the act of wearing it at an improper time, is ridiculous. A symmetrical child is beautiful ; but the sight of it in the hands of a demon, is revolting. Ornaments are beautiful, but increasing vanity by wearing them is disgusting.

It detracts more from the beauty of the inner temple than it adds to the fine appearance of the outer. An expensive, tasteful residence is beautiful. Yet if reared by means unlawfully gained, it is but a monument of shame to its builder.

That mode of dress is really the most beautiful, which while it is true to the laws of grace, is also true to the laws of health. To the philosophic mind, those passions which conflictwith the natural laws, are neither graceful nor beautiful. Health, being a powerful promoter of beauty, if in the arrangements of dress you disobey her laws, you are but bringing about the destruction of that beauty which you are laboring to promote. To admire beauty is inherent in every human breast. The child eagerly surveys her.

Gay colors, harmonious sounds, and gentle words, are not unheeded by the babe. They all possess an element of beauty which finds its echo even in the soul of a child.

Principles and actions are beautiful or otherwise, as they correspond with the divine elements of truth, love, wisdom. You cannot build beauty on slaughtered truth, or develop it on violated reason. It flourishes, when the electric connection between it and the entire sisterhood of virtues is unimpeded. Love, wisdom, knowledge, truth, grace, and beauty, are emanations from the same fountain of perfection : and who so seeks to increase beauty by trampling on any of these , will find himself baffled in his efforts. The natural laws are instituted to sustain all the virtues.

The love of the beautiful is not only right, but indispensable to the healthful progression of humanity. Yet, like the love of other things, it may be perverted. Faculties are perverted, when seeking to gratify themselves, they assume antogonistic relations to important principles. Thus, acquisitiveness is perverted, when it gratifies itself at the expense of honesty. Language is perverted, when it gratifies itself at the expense of charity. All cases of slander are instances of perverted language. Lips which should bless are laden with bitter words.

Amativeness is wofully perverted when trampling on reason, justice and benevolence it becomes the author of destruction to the unwary. Approbativeness is perverted, when it seeks to please man rather than God. Destructiveness is perverted, when directed toward truth rather than

error. Veneration is perverted, when it acts independently
of reason. Harmony of action is essential to purity of
action. Leave a faculty to act alone, and it disgraces
itself. Even reason insists on being accompanied by the
other faculties.

Without reason they have no director. Without them
she has no pupils and her province is to teach. The chief
danger in our love of beauty is that we make it a material
deity, administering almost exclusively to our physical
senses. Being a pervading element of every God like
principle, she has her dwelling place in reason, justice and
all the virtues. Her manifestations in material forms is
but the shadowing on the outer world of what exists in
the inner.

Were not beauty a constituent in the inner temple of
the Most-high, we should not behold it so gloriously shad-
owed in his works. We may not forget the giver, while
we admire the gift. Neither should we forget that it is an
element pervading all the graces, and that to adore it
apart from, and contrary to their precept, is to deprive it
of life, and hence of itself. Beauty can become mortal
only by ceasing to be itself. It is immortal, pervading
the celestial, eternal spheres with its exquisite presence.

Man from the combined action of constructiveness, ideality and reason, invents works of beauty. While reason
directs in the construction of the beautiful, it should also
direct in the use of the beautiful.

A feast may be got up at a great expense, and in a
most beautiful style. Though the outward of the feast is
beautiful, the sacrifice of principle which possibly it may
involve is hideous. It is well if it is sanctioned by all the
virtues. It is not well if it is given in the midst of poverty,
without regarding the sufferings of those who possess not

even the comforts of this mortal existence. It is not well, if it was instituted to gratify the inordinate action of alimentiveness. To make one's self sick at a feast is certainly not advisable. To our spirit perceptions, there seems a continuous chain of relations through all orderly existence. Break this chain and confusion is the result. When a young lady views her beauty as a thing peculiarly her own: as a thing for which she is to be praised and admired above others : when she allows her beauty to be prostituted, she forgets that beauty is divine and can flourish only in harmony with God-like elements. It is said that handsome persons are usually vain, seldom wise, and often immoral. When these conditions are manifest, it is because the individual becoming absorbed in the idea of his beauty, forgetting that beauty exists most perfectly with reason. Tear it from the graces to which it belongs, and like a branch separated from the vine, it withers and dies.

When the action of any faculty in the human organization favors the existence of an element opposed to beauty, beauty must retire in proportion to the degree in which the opposite element assumes the field. Would we cultivate beauty in its harmonious proportions, we must seek to know and obey the Creator's laws. It is meet that we walk in obedience, since obedience alone can insure to us happiness and the ever increasing pleasures of a higher life. Who does not desire to be obedient ? Who does not regret his former disobedience ! Who would not labor to bring all his powers into subjection to those laws, wisely instituted for his benefit? The spheres of light, love, and life, invite us to obedience, assuring us that it is the path to the wealth of immortality. Reason, veneration, conscience, hope, ideality, sublimity, and every exalted element of our nature is persuading us to obedience. Let us watch, pray and labor, until like practical Jesus, we have finished the work our Father has given us to do.

This world in which we live is a world of beauty ; but not of unmixed beauty. Disobedience must be subdued, before unmixed beauty shall strew its thornless flowers throuhgout our pathway. Beauty ! child of our Father's love ! we fold you to our hearts, imploring you to dwell there, in connection with all the divine principles which may dwell in the human heart. Some good people have been disaffected with material beauty. They have seen that to worship it in material things, is pernicious. Hence they have almost cast it out, as an enemy to man's spiritual good. Could they perceive the connection which exists between it and every holy principle, they would see that it is the admiring of it as an abstraction, which creates the difficulty.

Separating it from the vine of spiritual goodness, it loses its vitality, and in withering becomes an impure thing unfit to nourish man's spiritual and immortal nature.

INVOCATION.

Bands of the beautiful ! may we so live as to commune intimately with you. In the infusions of your purifying influences, may we be led to higher, holier planes of thought. While happy in the belief that the pure and beautiful are condescending to teach us, may we be equally glad to teach our brothers and sisters of a common humanity who may not yet have been favord with light equal to ours. We are desiring happiness and journeying to the world of realities. There, if not here, we shall see that the divine laws cannot be violated with impunity. Father save us in the spirit of obedience.

THOUGHTS ON IMMORTALITY.

Immortality, in its broadest, fullest sense, may be defined the continuous growth of life. Two of the most prominent results of life, are health and beauty : and as perfect health of body and mind cannot exist without balance or harmony throughout the physical and mental organization, so immortality in its full sense implies entire harmony of spiritual development. Immortality, in its full sense, also implies perfect beauty ; because unmixed beauty is the out-growth of harmony, unblemished, even by the smallest degree of irregularity.

Our Father will not accuse us of undue ambition in the selection of our theme, neither will he upbraid us for desiring fuller manifestations of the joys that await us on the shores of everlasting existence. We would not rend the vail, if we could, which hides from us the everlasting beauty of the everlasting hills ! but we would cultivate our souls, seeking to have them purified and renewed in strength, that they may perceive more and more of the wealth, beauty, and grandeur of the invisible world.

Saith scripture, "The things of the spirit are spiritually discerned. Eye hath not seen, nor ear heard, neither hath it entered into the heart of man to conceive the things which God hath prepared for them that love him. Nevertheless, he hath revealed them unto us by his spirit ; for the spirit searcheth all things ; yea the deep things of God." We read that there is a world of immortality. In our investigation of causes and relations, we conclude that there must be a world of immortality ; but in spirit only, do we feel that there is a world of immortality.

Foretastes of a glorious future, sometimes fill the believing with extatic joy; and in exchanging their mode of existence they have not unfrequently, broken the bars of the tomb, with songs of triumph and shouts of redemption and glory upon their lips. Can we doubt that the result of their faith, was a vision of the fadeless shore? Many have expressed themselves as beholding beings clad in light, waiting to convey them home. Many have heard singing, and some have seen, or though they saw chariots. Happy departures from earth are truly encouraging to us who yet reside in tenements of clay, teaching us of the power of Hope, Faith, Love, and Purity, to triumph over the last enemy: That the culture of all that is true and noble within us, will strengthen our souls for every conflict.

Divine revelation teaches the immortality of the soul; hence we infer that all the faculties thereof are immortal. When we talk of the human soul in connection with its immortality, we mean the human soul harmonious, existing in the divine image, according to our Father's ideal of a human soul. All perverted affections are in a spiritual sense, death to the soul. Inasmuch as they are permitted and nurtured, does the soul become a mass of corruption. Hence we read, "The soul that sinneth shall die." We do not expect that any of the pernicious elements or irregularities, woven into our soul-growth, will live or can live in heaven. We enjoy heaven here, so far as our souls are orderly, harmonizing with truth and righteousness. How sad a spectacle does the soul perverted exhibit. There are all the affections, all the intellectual facualties, and every element essential to the existence and growth of the soul. Reason is dethroned. The intellectual, moral, artistic, and kindly elements, are trampled upon by instinct, which was in the base of the brain to feed, serve, and empower the higher faculties. Instinct has assumed an improper position and claims to take the lead ; and alas ! it leads to the destruction of the organism, which in its true position, it would enrich with life, health and power. A soul thus disordered, is out of balance, and hence out of health, and being out of health, where is the guaranty of its life ? The diseased soul keenly suffers. Who would not strive for health of soul ? Disease of soul, sooner or later, leads to a loss of physical health. The life of man cannot die ; though his soul may be dead in trespasses and sins. The soul germ, imparted by Omnipotence to every human being, must live. It is Eternal, being an emanation from the Eternal, and so far as it becomes a permeater of the soul is it a sanctifier thereof. In some this germ seems sleeping in the depths of the soul, not having received light and heat congenial with itself, or what amounts to the same, not having received wisdom and love sufficient, to unfold and diffuse its beautiful power throughout the soul of its possessor. His surroundings have perhaps been of a withering, corrupting tendency. Yet the divine germ is there, constituting us all children of our Father, and Mother, God.

We read in the Bible that " God is the Father of all men, especially of such as believe." Said Jesus " He that liveth and believeth in me shall never die." Confidence places us in receptive conditions. We open our souls, because we expect to receive, while unbelief would shut them against the gift of our Father. The soul, as it is harmonized by the divine elements of love and wisdom, becomes angelic in the possession of orderly affections, and though an inhabitant of earth, by virtue of the material body, in spirit a communicant with the skies. We may not leave the Father, Son, and holy angels to do all that is to be done

for disorderly human spirits.   Each of us, in proportion to
the light we have received, have our work to do, and only
in doing cheerfully this work given us to do, can we become disciples of him who was obedient unto death.   I
consider it a crime to put our light under a bushel, or to
hide our talents in the earth.   They will die there : but in
the joys of an immortal existence, they will ever increase,
when properly used.   Said Jesus, " Not every one that
saith unto me Lord, Lord, shall enter into the kingdom of
heaven ; but he that doeth the will of my Father which is
in heaven."   Have we a neighbor, a friend, or even an enemy, who seems to us in need of help, and within the sphere
of our assistance, we should seek to impart to him the light
of truth and the warmth of love.   Inasmuch as we do good
to one of the least of the children of humanity, we do it to
Christ, who was, and who still is the great sympathizer
with human suffering, the result of conditions created by
human disobedience.   While we look to the Father, Son
and holy angels for our ministry, let us never neglect those
who seem often forgetful of this infinite source of benefit.
Sentiments of love and truth, uttered by the lips of a kind
friend, may prove effectual to lead the wanderer to the
fountain of light, love and life.

We believe that all the inherent faculties of the human
soul, will be retained and unfolded in the glorious world
of immortality.   What fields of knowledge for the intellectual powers to feed upon, may we expect to find in those
regions of eternal life.   Heaven would seem imperfect,
without the play of all those faculties, which are so essential to our happiness here.

Phrenologists having classed the elements of the human
mind into groups; we will consider each group separately,
in relation to its activity and use in spirit life.

First, the Perceptive Faculties. These are Form, Size, Equilibrium, Color, Order, Number, Eventuality, Locality and Time.

Language and Tune I place among the artistic elements, and not among the perceptives, as some phrenologists have done. What scope for the activity of Form, Size and Color, in combination with the artistic elements of Constructiveness, Ideality, and sublimity, do the majestic landscapes of the unseen world furnish.

We believe there are arbors and fountains, hills, planes, valleys, birds, flowers, and fruits, which are but faintly typified in this grosser world. We believe that all forms of beauty here are but faint pre-figurings of the forms or expressions of beauty there ; for as beauty is a spiritual element, existing in the divine mind, we must believe that expressions of beauty in the celestial and orderly spheres, are more real and intense than they can be here, where man has corrupted his ways. Father, draw us to paths of obedience, that our world may more abundantly bloom in health and beauty.

Equilibrium, Locality, Number and Order, must also find abundant scope in that world of varied beauty. Time, regarding condition and changes, must also be brought into use there. Probably it is not measured by seconds, minutes, hours, days, weeks, months and years, as we measure time here ; but marked by periods, states and progressions. The artistic elements called by some phrenologists the semi-intellectual faculties, we enumerate as Language, Tune, Imitation, Ideality, Sublimity and Constructiveness. These must find ample exercise in the blissful bowers of immortality. We believe that spirits there dwell in converse sweet, and ranging with the rapidity of thought over those floral planes, we doubt not that it is a source of high gratification to them to interchange ideas. We believe that the more developed are permitted to teach others. We do not pretend to say that they use spoken language, as we do, yet we doubt not that their language is more beautiful and comprehensive than we can here imagine. Being separated from diseased, material forms, their spiritual discernment is so quickened, that they are undoubtedly enabled to converse without audible expressions. Tune, or the faculty by which we appreciate and perform music, is undoubtedly a source of rich and unbounded pleasure in those regions of gladness. We can imagine the celestial world enraptured with refined and exalted symphonies. The very essence of music is there. Here we enjoy but the faint shadowing, of what exists there, in all its beautiful and sublime reality. Our most exquisite music here, but feebly echoing that of the spiritual, celestial spheres. We believe that persons who here were proficients in music, have there an unbounded field for the exercise of musical genius. We belive that Mozart and others, who were called from earth in the midst of arduous and beloved pursuits in this refining art and science, are most happy in finding the world of spirits beautifully. adapted to their further progression in this field of beauty and grandeur.

Constructiveness, an element of the all-pervading spirit, is also an element of the human soul. The Father's Constructiveness is manifested in the infinitude of his creations. Man's constructiveness is manifested in works of art, which contribute to his comfort and pleasure in this rudimental sphere.

Constructiveness is also important to a speaker or writer, as beauty and strength of language, imply the action of ingenuity or constructiveness, as well as of language.

Elegance of expression also calls into action the artistic power of imitation, as well as of Ideality and Sublimity.

Musicians and all artists, should possess Constructiveness full and active. So in the spirit world, that noble power will continue to unfold more and more. Some may inquire if we suppose that musicians there write music, as we do here. We do not by any means. We know little of that prospective world : but as we have before said, we believe it to be that which exists here only as shadowy and transitory. Shadows are fleeting. Realities are immortal. So our present existence is passing ; bringing us nearer and still nearer the promised land, where roses fade not and where music never ceases to charm. The reasoning, moral, and devout elements, must be vigorous there. The social nature in its varied manifesfations, will be there purified and exalted, but in no measure annihilated.

Did we love with devotion here, we shall love with purer devotion there. We believe friendship is an all-pervading element in those spheres of harmony, and love in her pure and exalted individuality, a beautifier of consonant spirits. What a glorious state ! not one faculty lost ; but all purified in increasing power.

> Upward we'll range those fields of pleasure,
> . Joying to know that still above,
> Are ever new and fadeless treasures,
> Gifts of our Father, full of love.
>
> Sad mourner, wish not back your brother,
> To tread with you these mortal shores.
> Prepare to join him in those mansions,
> Where sickness, grief and death are o'er.
>
> Fond parent, dry those tears of anguish :
> Your child lives in a brighter clime.
> Be pure in heart, and you shall meet him,
> Within those mansions, so divine.

Then call not back the soul departed !
  Though dear as life it was to thee.
Haste, haste, to meet it all immortal,
  When from these mortal shores you're free.

When fond ones leave us sad and lonely,
  Let us reflect, 'twill not be long,
Before like them, we cross the valley,
  And enter the immortal throng.

O ! let us strive to be quite ready,
  To hail the message with delight,
Which summons us from earth's dominions,
  Into the realms of endless life.

The element of Acquisitiveness must find pleasurable exercise there, in acquiring stores of love and wisdom Self-esteem, acting with veneration, affords pleasurable views of ourselves and others, as beings capable of continuous progression. Approbativeness, working delightfully with the elements of Reason and Conscience, makes us love to abide by all the divine laws, thus pleasing the All-wise and all-loving Father. The element of Secretiveness combined with Caution, acting with Reason and Justice, tends here to make people wise and prudent ; so there, the same powers find ample scope for action. The disembodied are not idly roaming those regions ; but are working. We presume they work without fatigue. They all have a mission, in the performance of which they require wisdom. Vita-tiveness, or tenacity of our present state of existence, is brought into use there. Beyond and above those fields on which the enfranchised soul first enters, there are those of grandeur so much greater, that it might neglect the present, in panting for the future, were it not restrained by the love of present existence. This power, acting with inhabitiveness, adhesiveness, and concentrativeness, keeps the

spirit attached to positions most favorable to its development, until it is prepared to rise higher. The propelling
and executive powers, including Combativeness and Destructiveness, are also necessary there to the soul's rapid
progression. Not acting as they often do here, as aggres-
sive forces, but in the power of appropriate courage, urging
the soul to higher and still higher planes of truth.

Immortality ! Theme beautiful and grand. The philos-
opher, poet and orator, may spend upon you their most en-
chanting expressions, and soon be obliged to retreat, for
the simple reason that language fails, and imagination
faints, while attempting to appreciate your delights. The
best eulogy we can bestow upon you, is to prepare for you.
What a delightful reflection that we all can call God our
Father, and feel assured that each, by virtue of birth, is
entitled to a share in the riches of immortality. Yet the
wealth of that country is wisely distributed. There is
nothing given to lie idly, or to be wasted in useless expenditure. We shall have all we can appreciate and use
wisely, and no more. The inheritance we shall receive on
entering there, will be proportionate to the preparation we
are in. Jesus has admonished us to lay up treasures in
immortality. Where can we obtain the treasures ? They
are from the bounty of our Father in heaven. The more
we watch and pray and work in the spirit of earnest obedience, the more abundant and beautiful are the treasures
which flow to the human heart from the divine. Do you ask
" Is God partial ? Why does he not bless all alike ?" He
does cause the sun to shine on all. He sends rain on all.
He robes the land in verdure, beauty and plenty. All who
can, may appreciate the beauty. All who labor may eat
of the fruits of that labor. Want exists in our world, not

because our Father has failed to bestow sources of comfort and also of luxury upon it. Human perversion, somewhere and somehow, is the cause of all the misery and all the want. Individuals who deserve a better lot, sometimes suffer the inconvenience of worldly poverty, from the inharmonies which exist, to a greater or less degree, throughout the present fabric of human society. Our Father bestows with an impartial hand the general blessings of the present existence. Particular blessings require adaptation in the recipient. The nature of spirit communion is extremely delicate. Material blessings for the material nature, are appreciated more or less by all men inhabiting the body. They are often craved to an unnecessary extent. One man pushes another off that he may have the more. Spiritual blessings must enter and become immortal treasures in the human soul, through a kind of agreement on the part of the recipient.

The soul must draw near to God. Says a materialistic friend, " God is all-pervading. How can I draw nearer ?" Friend, your question implies that you do not appreciate the delicacy of spiritual attractions and repulsions. Are you not aware of the interesting fact, that you may be in earnest conversation with another, and your spirits not mingle ? Minds and hearts mingle, only in the degree in which they become adapted to each other, or in which they become capable of assimilating with each other. We do not say they must be alike, but simply that they must possess attraction, or as chemists express it, affinity for each other.

The human soul in order to be receptive of the divine elements of love and wisdom, must be passive ; a willing pupil of the infinite mind. I will and I wont, have no place in him who would be taught. The soul submissive, must have full confidence in the almighty teacher. Confidence in the laws, by which he would control and keep his entire creation in the most perfect order. Our Father's government ever leaves man free to act ; but not free to choose the consequences of his actions. Our Father does not compel us to obey his laws. If he did, there would be no virtue on our part, in obedience. He invites us into paths of obedience, assuring us that they are the true paths, and that in walking in them, we shall not be disappointed in our expectations of peace here and hereafter. If we do not obey the divine laws, whether we will or not, we *must* suffer the penalty which always exist in the corresponding action. Repeated acts of disobedience stamp upon the soul their blighting impression, and so harden the naturally sensitive soul, that it becomes unconcerned in the midst of perversions at which once it would have recoiled. The individual is miserable ; and seems not to know why. Repeated acts of disobedience, have blinded the understanding, as well as corrupted the moral nature.

O! let us turn from paths so dark and wretched ;
From cheerless marshes whence corruptions rise.
The sun of hope is gracing the horison,
And light all pure, is beaming from the skies,

Mortal, your spirit lives to be immortal !
O! do not quench it in it's upward flame :
Help it by truth divine, to gain the portal,
Where toiling spirits do not faint again.

Skill, power, truth, wisdom and love unbounded,
In all the Father's matchless laws do shine.
We'll see the wisdom, while we share the blessing,
Of firm obedience to the will divine.

Here, let us seek to walk in sweet subjection,
Knowing the all perfect cannot be unkind :
What'er he wills, with gladness let us welcome,
We'll see the cause when we our heaven find.

All will be well, if we but walk in order:
To strict obedience the reward is sure,
The great, celestial portals ever open,
To welcome spirits, contrite, constant, pure.

To lay up treasures in heaven, is to store the soul with sentiments and purposes of love and wisdom. These purposes, when they are real, manifest themselves (as far as circumstances will permit) in actions. "The tree is known by its fruit. A tree which bears excellent fruit, we expect to bear more excellent fruit, when transplanted into a richer soil. The object in transplanting is not to change the kind, but to improve the quality. A pear tree will not become an apple tree, but simply a better pear tree, by removing it to a richer soil. So, if here, we carefully cultivate our souls, seeking to attract to them pure, immortal elements, we shall have them laid up as treasures in the kingdom of heaven within us. We shall find them bright and fadeless in the world of immortality, where moth and rust do not corrupt, and where thieves do not break through nor steal." Spiritual attainments, mental growth and wealth, are worthy of attention, since they are immortal. Deck the material form in robes of beauty, and they soon become faded and worn. Not so with robes of spiritual beauty. They grow brighter for the wearing. True mental culture sickens and dies not, when the frail tenement of clay sickens and dies. The soul retains all the truth and all the beauty, that it has atracted to itself in this rudimental sphere. In the impressive words of Long-fellow,

" Let us then be up and doing,
With a heart for any fate :
Still achieving, still pursuing,
Learn to labor and to wait.

Life is real : life is earnest :
And the grave is not it's goal.
Dust thou art, to dust returnest,
Was not spoken of the soul."

The power of firmness is very important in human character. We think it will lose none of its effectiveness in the
future world Acting with concentrativeness, it will keep the
spirit loyal to every trust, and victoriously achieving every
undertaking. No weariness or fainting there ; but eternal health, activity, and beauty. Stores of infinite life are
the inheritance of the immortal spirit. We should not
crowd ourselves here, or impair our health by overdoing.
The cycles of unending ages are before us. Yet it is all
important that this, our rudimental existence, be diligently
improved. As mind in the outer world, operates through
the physical faculties, to crowd the mind beyond physical
capacity, must destroy the harmony which we should aim
to promote between mind and body.

To make our mental achievements profitable to our co-
temporaries, we need sufficient strength of physical organization, to constitute us good conductors for the unfolding
power of the soul. We may possess minds equal to those
of Franklin or Newton ; but if the physical system is weak
or diseased, we shall fail to act with the efficiency which
would otherwise characterize us. Strong minds in weak,
diseased bodies, pass into the spiritual sphere, without
having done in the outer world half that they would have
done, under more favorable conditions. However the weak

should not repine ; but do the best they can to preserve harmony between body and soul.

The day of deliverance draws near. We should not despise the body. It is the spirit's agent. Neither need we fear to emerge from it, when it is unable to serve longer.

> What we term death is but a change,
> A transit of the soul ;
> A living on in endless life,
> The spirit's friendly goal.

INVOCATION.

Holy Father, we would remember that the present life is the commencment of our immortality. We would live purely. Live to do good. Live to grow strong in spirit. Live not to ourselves ; but to him who died for us and rose again. In living to him and for the perpetuity of his ministry, we shall live in love and peace, and according to our ability, in active service to our race. Then we need not fear to tread the pathway to a higher life. Jesus has blessed it ; and is ever waiting to welcome the obedient to the joys of the spiritual world.

PART THIRD.

———⚘———

Spirit Voices from the

BELOVED DEPARTED to SURVIVING FRIENDS,

FIRST VOICE.

No. 1.

Farewell to the links which bound me to earth,
I dwell in the regions where love had its birth.
No longer I wander with heart heavy and sad,
With longings and sighings to be cheerful and glad :
I dwell in the region of knowledge and truth,
And bask in the beauty of unfading youth.
I would not again be encased in clay :
Though you do not behold me, I'm with you to-day ;
And at noon, and at evening's sweet, hallowed hours,
I come and enwreath you with beautiful flowers,
When sadly you're mourning my absence on earth,
Remember, I'm dwelling where LOVE had its birth.

Calm be your souls ! prepared for the hour,
When over you also, the propitious power
Which teachers of old, have termed *death*, shall arise,
To bear you to dwell with the good and the wise ;
O ! cease all your mourning my absence on earth,
I dwell in the region where love had its birth.

Farewell ! but not forever ;
  For to each loved one, I bring
And place upon the finger
  A pure and signet ring ;
A pledge that I'll be with you
  While you of earth remain,
And lovingly will greet you,
  In the spirit world again.

No. 2.

'Tis sweet to rest the form in mother earth ;
To enter into spirits' higher birth.
The soul regrets past follies, it is true,
And on truth's altar it begins anew.

O ! happy hour which first did welcome me,
To listen to the spirit minstrelsy ;
My soul absorbed, forgot its care and pride,
With guardian angels ever by my side.

They had always watched over my steps,
Would that I'd known it, but I'll not regret—
The past has been reviewed, ail wrong forgiven,
And never sighing more I dwell in heaven.

Waiting to welcome to this fairer clime,
The darling friend, who loved me so in time ;
The mother's yearning love, and father's care,
And precious more than all, their humble prayer

Have not been lost. Rich treasures ! they were given
In pain to bring me to the birth of heaven.
And when again I pen some thoughts to you,
They shall be of the beautiful and true.

Casting away the shadows of the past,
While as we journey on, we firmly grasp,
The loving, beautiful, and pure and true ;
I'm with you, ever on your way pursue,

Until we meet in richer bowers above,
Where every action is a proof of love.

No. 3.

Our loved ones in Earth life are passing along,
And the time of re-union cannot be long ;
Our hearts swell with joy when we think of the hour,
Which shall bear you in peace to our beautiful bower.

The soul all immortal cannot sleep in the clay,
I'm with you in spirit, not in Oakwood* to day ;
The emblems there planted which are green all the year,
Speak gently, sad mourners, we bid you not fear,
* Oakwood Cemetery, Syracuse, N. Y.

For your loved onces departed, cannot sleep in the clay,
They are with *you* in spirit, not in *Oakwood* to-day ;
The emblems there planted are *your souls* to cheer,
For the plants of our kingdom do bloom all the year.

No. 4.

You may not mourn my absence, for I am with you still ;
And when you feel this fully, I can your spirit fill,
With a measure of the calmness, the peace, and joy and love
Which ever come meandering from higher courts above.

And you'll be happy mother, when your soul is reconciled,
And feel my presence with you, your own, your darling chid,
And we will clasp hands mother, and each the other greet,
With even more affection than we were wont to meet.

No. 5.

When morning o'er the earth her brilliant carpet throws,
And sweetly, gaily bloom, the lily and the rose,
Do you think me far away from your loving hearts so true ?
Ah no ! I'm with you then, and I'll ever dwell with you,

For in these sunny isles, far, far beyond the sea,
Which you of Earth call death, I live all bright and free ;
I bring you flowers of love, and flowers of wisdom too ;
I am not far away, but ever dwell with you.

Then bright and happy be in your earth home so fair,
Let woes be forgot in humble, trusting prayer ;
Our Father is so good He doeth all things well !
Let this thought fill your hearts with joy, words cannot tell.

And yet loved ones all, it gives me joy to know,
That you on me so oft, do thoughts of love bestow ;
That you often think of me with affection's tears ;
O ! let this much suffice, and banish all your fears.

You no more should mourn for me so blessed as I ;
Escaped from every snare, and beyond the sky,
Of discord, care and pain, from sin forever free ;
I wait with joy to greet the friends who think of me.

SECOND VOICE.

FROM A YOUNG LADY.

I'm waiting for you mother,
In spheres of bliss above ;
Where we know not pain in parting,
Though hearts are full of love.

Our souls no more in anguish,
Pass dreary hours away :
We're dwelling in the light, mother,
Of everlasting day.

You we often visit,
And labor to impress,
Your stricken heart with calmness,
And lead your soul to rest.

Blooming bowers, mother,
Of beauty, love, and truth,
Are now for you preparing,
Here you'll renew your youth.

Now your soul is rising
From the weight it did bear ;
For patient and confiding,
It has became in prayer.

The drear past, dear mother,
Let us put far away ;
It may no longer haunt us,
In this pure clime of day.

Neither on earth, mother,
Should it your joy consume ;
Your souls should dwell in gladness,
As *we* do beyond the tomb.

We bring floral emblems
Of all that's true and fair ;
To wreathe your souls in beauty,
And make you happy there.

O ! could you know the love,
We on your soul do shed ;
The care with which we guard you,
You would soon raise your head,

To droop no more in anguish ;
For spheres of light and truth,
Could come so near your spirit,
As to make it bright like youth.

Though blessed with experience
Which many years have given,
The thorns would be extracted,
And your soul bloom in heaven.

Then upward rise, mother,
And brighter grow each day ;
All pleasant things remember,
But the *dark past put away.*

THIRD VOICE.

FROM A YOUNG LADY.

Mine was a happy life, mother,
 I knew not much sorrow or care ;
I gathered bright flowers growing near me,
 And wove many sweet garlands fair.

I grasp'd the fond hand of friendship,
 And love was not strange to my heart.
I danced in a fountain of pleasure,
 Not dreaming but that it would last.

My morning so bright and happy,
 Grew brighter, as higher it rose ;
Advancing toward noonday meridian,
 When a tempest foretold its close.

That storm so shook our bark, mother,
  You trembled and could not be calm ;
I arose on the pinions of angels,
  And harbored remote from alarm.

The wise and loving conveyed me
  To this boundless haven of bliss ;
And wisely they watch o'er the changes
  Less known in your world, than in this.

For change gives breadth to the spirit,
  And opens wide fountains of joy.
It raises us higher in wisdom,
  And frees us from spurious alloy.

I would come nearer dear mother,
  When you weep to drive sadness away,
And to deck you in garlands of beauty,
  Whenever in anguish you pray.

I'm sad in seeing your sadness,
  Dear mother, be happy like me ;
Earth would be an eden of beauty,
  Were its children unselfish and free.

Know that I still live to bless you,
  And to draw you nearer to me ;
As you on the wings of progression,
  From sadness are aiming to flee.

Bright winged teachers, my mother,
  Would have you all happy and free ;
For they by the power of progression,
  Are bringing your nearer to me.

FOURTH VOICE.

FROM A YOUNG SOLDIER WHO RECEIVED DEATH-WOUNDS IN BATTLE.

I'm far away from the planes I trod,
　From the field of war and blood ;
The banner of peace waves over my head,
　And I'm harbored with my God.

No more I hear the bugle sound,
　To summon men to strife ;
I'm in the summer land so fair,
　And drink of the springs of life.

Dear, loving ones who bravely bore
　The tidings of my doom,
My heart is with you now, as when
　You watched my boyhood's bloom.

And nearer still I come to you,
　When you are bowed in prayer,
And whisper thoughts of hope and peace,
　And loving angel's care.

I bravely fought—I bravely fell
　For the country held so dear,
And you dear ones have bravely strove
　To dry the gushing tear.

And think of me with thoughts of peace,
　Sweet resignation's power,
To you celestial comfort gives,
　In every trying hour.

Such bravery shall be recompensed
  In brighter world above ;
When we, a happy band, shall meet
  Around the throne of Love.

FIFTH VOICE.

FROM A LADY.

Loved ones, we're dwelling in gladness,
  On this balmy, beautiful shore ;
Three sisters, united forever,
  In a sphere where grief is no more.

I never had dreamed of the beauty,
  Which ever unfolds in this clime ;
Where our teachers of love and of wisdom,
  Help us every woe soon to resign.

I would not return to the cold world,
  To languish in sorrow and pain ;
Though Ive passed from your sight dearest Parents;
  Your loss is my infinite gain.

The world seemed to me cold and heartless ;
  And thorns in my pathway were strewn ;—
But now I have passed far above them,
  To a sphere where strife is unknown.

The calm, peaceful waters of Freedom ;
  The sweet air of Justice and Peace ;
And the bright flowers of Truth blooming round me,
  Is not this a happy release ?

O ! join in my anthem of praises,
 To the giver of infinite life ;
Death to me was a flood-gate of blessing,
 For it lead me from sorrow and strife.

THE SHINING SHORE.

AN ADDITIONAL POEM FROM THE FIRST VOICE.

Can I describe the Shining Shore,
Where moments of sadness forever are o'er?
Can I sing of this land of light?
Can mortal language express the delight,
Which ever unfolds in this land of the blest,
Where the faintest and saddest find comfort and rest?
  I'll try, though words poorly express
   The scenes of this brilliant shore ;
  And yet they may lead your mind to dwell,
   On beauties unthought of before.
This Shining Shore is a scene of repose,
Where the spirit casts off its load of woes :
And dwells in light serene and pure,
In the midst of pleasures which ever endure.
  Here are gems so bright !
  Here is a constant flood of light !
  Here are pearls so clear,
   And flowers which bloom throughout the year.
The roseate hue of gladness o'er you steals,
When thinking of the radiance of this shore :
And its pure inspirations
   On you pour.

Inhaling its rich truths in a degree,
Your soul grows strong, your spirit bright and free.
Here is no age, but that of true development.
Wrinkles are lost, and care-worn looks exchanged
      For smiles of joy.
  O ! live in freedom, love and truth,
    Till Earth become a shining shore,
  Where mortals tread
    In pleasures evermore.
  Not pleasures of a low consuming power,
  Pleasures of sense which wither in an hour ;
  But these conformed to wisdom's priceless plan,
  Given to enhance the eternal peace of man.
Here Milton ranges in his thought sublime,
And Cowper ample scope here finds for Rhyme.
Melancthon in Theology does roam,
And Shakspeare finds in richer Plays *his* home.
Mozart in Music revels with delight,
And Washington's great theme is Human Right.
John Howard, visits yet the prisoner's cell,
And seeks unfortunates where'er they dwell.
Joan of Arc with noble warrior's power,
Holds truth and virtue steadfast every hour.
Ne'er swerves from duty on the shining planes,
For sure she did it well in earth's domains.
And spirits of great truth and justice, never
Lose in these points, when from the form they sever :
While those of virtue less, in these bright climes
May choose the right, and all their sins resign.
They cannot downward grow mid truth so clear,
They must receive of virtue, when so near
She comes to them with Love and Wisdom true,
They must exchange the dark *past* for the new

The bright and shining garments of the free.
Who can resist the fruits of life's fair tree?
True, some are long in learning to explore
The mines of wealth, which from truth's sources pour;
But all at length must come to know full well,
The priceless riches of salvation's well.
Rejoice with me ! Its waters cleanse my soul.
And make me upright stand in self-control,
Through power divine to you in truth I come,
To tell you of the glories of my home,
And many whom I learned much to admire,
Milton and Byron, Shakespeare, clothed in fire
Of poetry and music, deign to come
And grace with truth and harmony your home.
Spirits of greatness on this shining shore,
Words cannot name them; they are legion, sure.
When poets enter these immortal planes
They cease their rhyming for sweet music strains
Musicians turn their thougths to painting fine
And sculpture in its turn absorbs the mind.
For in earth life, few can at once excel
In all these gifts, though they within them dwell.
These changes are for growth, and when complete
Each revels most in that to him most sweet.
All study mind. The laws which it control
Is the great study for the human soul.
Whether in earth life, or in higher state,
It only can make human beings great.
Great in good deeds and in sweet charity :
It makes man upright, courteous and free.
Respect unto the least of human kind
Is the true index of a noble mind.
And dearest ones the love I cherished

Has brighter grown on this sweet shore ;
And in devotion still increasing,
It links me to you evermore.

Why linger by the grave,
As though I could be there ?
All that made that form
Living, bright, and fair,
Has passed to higher life ;
A spirit body wears.

I linger by the grave,
But in it enter not;
I only hear your sobbings,
Telling I'm not forgot.
I fain would reach my hand,
And wipe away the tears :
I'd whisper to your spirit,
Soothing away its fears ;
I'd bid you tearless, fearless press,
To this immortal shore,
Where the grave is lost in victory,
And triumph evermore.

Beauty is so abundant
On this delightful shore,
We gaze and gaze upon it,
And could scarcely wish for more.

When lo ! it comes so richly,
Bringing a fervent glow
Of such sublime rejoicing,
As mortals never know.

We must become immortal,
    Ere we can be prepared
For visions of the beautiful,
    Treasured in our reward.

Stored for those who labor,
    To gain the heights of truth ;
They're stored for those who love
    With the innocence of youth.

Of childhood not perverted,
    Of youth not linked with wrong ;
The beautiful, the beautiful,
    Shall finish our glad song.

We see it in the rivulets
    Of this immortal shore :
In chrystal drops of glowing light,
    It comes forevermore.

They are the dew-drops of our land,
    Making our flowrey lawns
Such scenes of varied beauty,
    As never Earth adorn.

But ah ! you have enough on earth
    For the rudimental sphere,
The earthly form could never bear,
    The pleasures we taste here.

The soul would break its casket
    Amid supreme delight ;
And soar to these blest regions
    Of everlasting light.

Then cherish all the beautiful
  Our Father gives to earth :
And all the inspiration
  Which is of heavenly birth.

Soon shining bands will meet you,
  And greet you on this shore;
Where beauty in abundance,
  Will bless you evermore.